Molly had a **magic** place,
Where she would go to play.

She found it in her Granny's house,
One cold and rainy day . . .

MOLLY'S MAGIC WARDROBE

Search for the Fairy Star

Adam & Charlotte Guillain

Garry Parsons

One day when she was playing,
Molly found some sparkly things.
"A fairy costume!" Molly gasped,
"With shiny golden wings!"

She climbed in Granny's wardrobe,
Swished the clothes back with her hand,

And with a shower of stars
She **whizzed away** to . . .

…Fairyland!

"Hello!" a fairy called, "I'm Flo.
I'm in an *awful* fix.
My wand has lost its star and now
I can't do spells or tricks."

"I'll help you find it!" Molly said.

"Let's try behind this door . . ."

They stepped inside a castle,
And they crept across the floor.

"My star's not here," said Fairy Flo.
"But look at those **huge eyes!**"

Molly cried, "Don't panic!" as . . .

. . . a giant said,

"Surprise!"

"Please don't be scared!" he told them.

"I'm the nicest giant by far."

"Then could you help us?" Molly said.

"Flo's lost her magic star."

The giant frowned and scratched his head.

"I know what might be good!

I bet your star is hiding

In the dark, enchanted wood."

They fluttered to the twisted trees,
And landed on the ground.
They didn't see a shadow loom
Or hear a **rustling** sound.

Then, suddenly . . .

. . . a big grey WOLF
Sprang out and blocked their way!
"Please don't be scared!" he told them,
"I'm not bad, like people say."

Molly said, "Flo's lost her star.
We're searching everywhere."

"Aha!" the wolf said. "Have you tried
That garden over there?"

They ran into the garden . . . .

. . . and a **witch** swooped overhead!

"Please don't be scared!" she told them.
"Do you like my flowerbed?"

"It's lovely," Molly smiled, "But have
You seen Flo's star round here?"
The witch looked sad and shook her head.
Flo sighed and shed a tear.

But Molly cried, "Flo, listen!

Do you hear that tinkling bell?"

She led Flo through the garden
Where they found . . .

. . . a Wishing well!

The two friends quickly made a wish.

Then, in a **flash** of light,
A magic silver star appeared
And twinkled, clear and **bright**.

"It's **magic** time!" cheered Fairy Flo.

"Hurray for wishing wells!"

She waved her wand and Molly gasped

At all her **tricks** and spells.

Fireworks fizzed and **whooshed** and **whizzed**,

Cakes dropped down from the sky!

They sat down to a fairy tea,

As unicorns flew by!

"Thank you, Flo," said Molly.

"Can you grant me one more wish?

I'd like to go **back home** now."

So Flo gave her wand a swish...

Molly landed
in the wardrobe,
Where she got a
big surprise . . .

For hanging
round her neck
she found . . .

A shining fairy prize.

"Thank you, Flo," she whispered
As she put the clothes away.
"And, goodbye, magic wardrobe,
I'll be back another day."

For Elisa – A. & C. Guillain

For Codie & Kyle – G.P.

How to assemble your wings

1. Ask a grown-up to help you.

2. Push the small cardboard
circles out of the wings.

3. Feed two long pieces of ribbon through the
holes and tie the ends of the ribbon together.

4. Your magical fairy wings are ready to wear!

EGMONT
We bring stories to life

First published in Great Britain 2018 by Egmont UK Limited, The Yellow Building, 1 Nicholas Road, London W11 4AN

www.egmont.co.uk

Text copyright © Adam & Charlotte Guillain 2018
Illustrations copyright © Garry Parsons 2018

The moral rights of the authors and illustrator have been asserted.

ISBN 978 1 4052 8525 4